BETHAN STEVENS

The Not-So-Wicked Witch

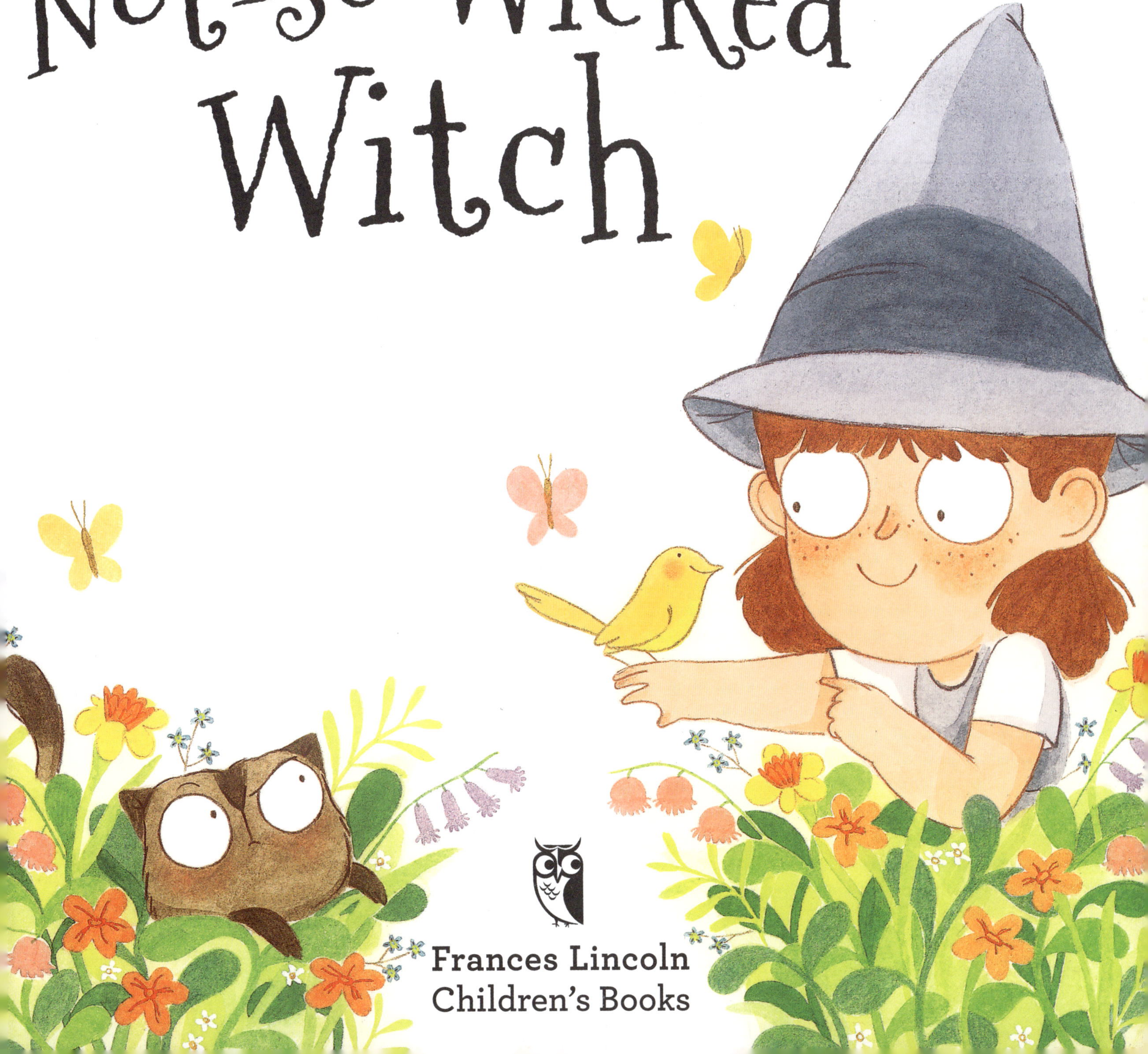

Frances Lincoln
Children's Books

On the sleepiest of nights,
when the air is still and the moon
is full, conditions are just right . . .
for witches to take flight!

What a **terrible** bunch they are!

I know, as well you do, that witches are wicked through and through.

Ever stepped on a pointy toy
with bare feet?

A **witch** put it there.

Ever gone to eat
the last biscuit
only to find the
jar is empty?

A **witch** ate the last one.

Ever wondered why you
can only find **one** of
your favourite socks?

A **witch** pinched the other one.

Just. For.
Fun.

But in amongst all this wickedness is a bit of a surprise. Because although this one,

and
this one,

and even **the cats**
(don't let their sweet faces fool you)
are **wicked** . . .

. . . this one is
surprisingly **nice!**

This is the littlest witch,
and she doesn't enjoy being
wicked like the others.

She is **helpful**

and **thoughtful**

with kindness
in her heart.

How confusing for the other witches!
They simply can't understand what good
could come of being sweet and kind.

The other witches decide the littlest witch needs rescuing from all this icky, gooey goodness! It's time for some lessons in wickedness.

For an excellent day of wickedness, you begin with a little light troublemaking in the morning.

Continue with a healthy helping of mischievous magic at the dinner table.

And finish with a good dose of naughtiness at bedtime.

But all the littlest witch wants to do is be kind and make friends.

The wicked witches are beginning to think there's no hope for our littlest witch.

But wait, what's this?
A birthday party?!
The most perfect place
for a spot of wickedness!

There's bunting . . .
excitable children . . .
presents . . . and do
I spy marsh—

It is a little known fact that witches love nothing more in the world than marsh—

So, these naughty, wicked witches hatch a plan to steal the tasty marshmallows and teach the littlest witch her most important lesson yet.

If nothing else, the littlest witch has to be good at this. The wicked witches give the littlest witch a list of ingredients because it's time to show some wickedness.

The littlest witch **loves** marshmallows just as much as the other witches. But it doesn't feel right to steal them! And it's not exactly easy collecting the sneeze of a shrew . . .

or a grumpy toad . . .

or the hair
from a wiry hog.

The littlest witch is about to give up when suddenly she has an idea – one that will help get the marshmallows a different way . . .

And with her special ingredients gathered,
she flies off to make her potion.

The witches do their magic dance
around the cauldron as the littlest
witch mixes the potion . . .

Little witches we may be,
but don't be fooled by what you see!
Though we're not the biggest lot,
our spells are strong, our cauldron hot.
With worm and shrew and mud and toads,
we'll cast a spell to make them doze!
And once the yummy treats are gone,
off we'll fly, our day is done!

A happy day is a wicked day.
That's what little witches say!

When the potion is ready, the littlest witch turns it into a delicious cake – the perfect treat for a wicked birthday celebration.

And when no one is looking the little witches creep in and SWITCH the birthday cakes.

The wicked little witches all hide, giggling with anticipation while they wait for the children to eat their cake and fall asleep so they can steal the marshmallows.

Before the wicked witches can stop her,
the littlest witch jumps out from her
hiding place and says,

The wicked witches turn to their littlest friend with frowns on their faces . . .

But to their
surprise, all of
the children begin
to clap and cheer.

And as a thank you for the delicious cake,
the birthday girl welcomes all the little witches
to the party and offers them some cake . . .

and

MARSHMALLOWS,

of course.

And the wicked little witches learn
that the littlest witch was right all along –
kindness beats wickedness . . .

Well, most of the time.

For Elspeth

First Published in 2024 by Frances Lincoln Children's Books,
an imprint of The Quarto Group.
1 Triptych Place, London, SE1 9SH, United Kingdom.
T (0)20 7700 6700 F (0)20 7700 8066 **www.Quarto.com**

A catalogue record for this book is available from the British Library.
ISBN 978-0-7112-7599-7

The illustrations were created using watercolour
Set in IM FELL French Canon and Romp Pro

Designer: Zoë Tucker
Production Controller: Dawn Cameron
Senior Commissioning Editor: Claire Grace
Art Director: Karissa Santos
Publisher: Peter Marley

Manufactured in Guangdong, China, TT052024
1 3 5 7 9 8 6 4 2

MIX
Paper | Supporting responsible forestry
FSC® C016973